CHILDREN'S
STORYTIME COLLECTION

Jimbo Comes Home

AND OTHER STORIES

Contents

DP
DEMPSEY
PARR

Jimbo Comes Home

Jimbo the circus elephant was snoring away in his cage one night when he heard a strange noise. At first he thought it was part of his dream. In his dream he was walking across a hot, dusty plain while in the distance there was the sound of thunder.

All at once Jimbo was wide awake. He realized that he was in his cage after all and that what he thought was the sound of thunder was the noise of his cage on the move. Now this worried him, because the circus never moved at night. He rose to his feet and looked around. He could see men pulling on the tow bar at the front of the cage. These were strangers – it certainly wasn't Carlos his trainer! Jimbo started to bellow, "Help! Stop thief!" But it was too late. His cage was already rumbling out of the circus ground and down the road.

Eventually, the cage passed through a gate marked 'Zipper's Circus' and Jimbo knew what had happened. He had been stolen by the Zipper family, his own circus family's greatest rivals! Jimbo was furious. How had the thieves got away with it? Surely someone at Ronaldo's Circus must have heard them stealing him? But Jimbo waited in vain to be rescued.

The next morning, the thieves opened up Jimbo's cage and tried to coax him out, but he stayed put. In the end, after much struggling, they managed to pull him out. Once he was out of his cage, he took the biggest drink of water he could from a bucket and soaked his new keeper! He refused to cooperate, kicked over his food, and when he appeared in the circus that night he made sure he got all the tricks wrong.

"Don't worry," said Mr Zipper to Jimbo's new trainer, "he'll just take a little while to settle down. Soon he'll forget that he was once part of Ronaldo's Circus." But Jimbo didn't forget for, as you know, an elephant never forgets.

The other animals in Zipper's Circus had all been stolen from other circuses, too. "You'll just have to get used to it here," said one of the chimps to Jimbo. "It's not so bad really." But Jimbo decided he was going to try and escape.

One night, a mouse passed by his cage. "Hello," called Jimbo mournfully, for by now he was feeling very lonely, and no-one had cleaned his cage out for days.

"Hello!" said the mouse. "You don't look very happy. What's the matter?" Jimbo explained how he had been stolen and wanted to escape back to his own circus. The mouse listened and then said, "I'll try to help." So saying, he scampered off and soon he was back with a bunch of keys. Jimbo was astonished. "Easy!" said the mouse. "The keeper was asleep, so I helped myself."

Jimbo took the keys in his trunk and unlocked the door to the cage. He was free! "Thank you!" he called to the mouse, who was already scurrying away.

Jimbo's first thought was to get back to his own circus as fast as possible. However, he wanted to teach those thieves a lesson. He could hear them snoring in their caravan. He tiptoed up, as quietly as an elephant can tiptoe, and slid into the horse's harness at the front. "Hey, what do you think you're doing?"

neighed one of the horses, but Jimbo was already hauling the robbers' caravan out of the gate and down the road.

So gently did he pull the caravan that the thieves never once woke up. Eventually they reached Ronaldo's Circus. Mr Ronaldo was dumbstruck to see Jimbo pulling a caravan just like a horse! Mr Ronaldo walked over to the caravan and was astonished to see the robbers still fast asleep. He raced to the telephone and called the police, and it wasn't until they heard the police siren that the robbers woke up. By then it was too late. As they emerged from the caravan scratching and shaking their heads they were arrested on the spot and taken off to jail. "There are a few questions we would like to ask Mr Zipper regarding the theft of some other circus animals, too," said one of the police officers.

Mr Ronaldo, and Jimbo's keeper Carlos, were both delighted to see Jimbo back home again. And Jimbo was just as delighted to be back home. Then Mr Ronaldo and Carlos started whispering to each other and began walking away looking secretive. "We'll be back soon, we promise," they said to Jimbo. When they returned, they were pushing Jimbo's old cage. It had been freshly painted, there was clean, sweet-smelling straw inside, but best of all there was no lock on the door! "Now you can come and go as you please," said Carlos.

And Jimbo trumpeted long and loud with his trunk held high, which Carlos knew was his way of saying, "THANK YOU!"

The Bee Who Wanted More Stripes

Bertie the bee was a rather vain young bee. Every morning, as soon as he woke up, he would find a large dewdrop in which to admire his reflection. The thing that Bertie liked best about himself was his stripes. He thought stripes were the smartest and most striking fashion accessory any animal could have. He just wished he had more stripes. But he only had a couple. "Still," he thought, "they are very fine stripes."

Then he had an idea. What if he could get some more stripes? He would be the stripiest bee around, and then everyone else would admire him, too. "I know what I'll do," he said. "I'll ask some other very stripy animals how they got all their stripes, and maybe I can copy them."

He buzzed off through the wood, looking for striped animals to ask. He flew across the fields and then the sea and at last he reached a place where there seemed to be quite a few striped animals. The first animal he approached looked like a striped horse. "Hello, neddy!" said Bertie, landing on the beast's nose.

"I'm not a horse – I'm a zebra. And get off my nose!" said the zebra crossly.

"I do beg your pardon," said Bertie. "I just wanted to ask you how you got your stripes."

"Well," said the zebra, "I used to be all brown. Then one day I came across a piano in the middle of the plain. As I walked past the piano, its black and white keys started to play a tune all by themselves. Then I looked down and found I had turned black and white, too. And if you believe that you'll believe anything!" And with that the zebra laughed and trotted off.

Bertie continued on his way. Now he could see a large striped cat. "Hello, puss!" said Bertie, landing on the creature's back.

"I'm not a cat – I'm a tiger. And get off my back!" growled the tiger.

"I'm so sorry," said Bertie, "I just wanted to ask you how you got your stripes."

"Well," said the tiger, "I used to be all yellow. Then one day, when I was a cub, I was playing with a ball of black string and I got all tangled up in it. And that's how I got my stripes. And if you believe that you'll believe anything!" And the tiger started to laugh as he stalked off.

Bertie continued on his way. Soon he could see a long striped worm slithering through the grass. "Hello, little worm!" called Bertie, landing on the worm's tail.

"I'm not a worm – I'm a snake. And get off my tail!" hissed the snake.

"Oh dear. I didn't mean to upset you," said Bertie. "I just wanted to ask you how you got your stripes."

"Well," said the snake, "I used to be all brown. Then one day I was crossing a road just as the traffic lights were changing from red to green, and when I reached the other side I found that I was striped red and green from head to tail. And if you believe that you'll believe anything!" And the snake started to laugh as he slithered away.

Bertie continued on his way once more. Then he spotted a squirrel with a striped tail in a tree. "Hello, squirrel!" he said, landing on the animal's paw.

"I'm not a squirrel – I'm a ring-tailed lemur. And get off my paw!" said the ring-tailed lemur angrily.

"I do apologise," said Bertie. "I just wanted to ask you how you got your striped tail."

11

"Well," said the ring-tailed lemur, "my tail used to be all white. Then one day I was playing hoop-la with my friends. I said they could use my tail as a target, and so they threw all the rings on to my tail. But they got stuck. And that's how I got a striped tail. And if you believe that you'll believe anything!" And the ring-tailed lemur started to laugh as he scampered away.

"Well," thought Bertie, "I'd better give it a go!" First he looked for a piano on the plain, but to no avail. There just wasn't a piano to be found. Then he looked for a ball of string – but he couldn't find one of those, either. He did find a set of traffic lights and he buzzed backwards and forwards in front of them until he felt quite dizzy, but he still had the same number of stripes. Finally, he called out, "Anyone fancy a game of hoop-la?" But there was no reply. It was night time and all the animals were asleep.

"I'll just have to make my way home," thought Bertie sadly. He flew all through the night and arrived home exhausted in the morning.

Just then he met Clarice, the wise old bee. "Clarice," said Bertie, "I really would like some more stripes, but although I've asked lots of stripy animals how they got their stripes, all they gave me were silly answers."

Clarice looked at Bertie rather sternly and said, "You only get the stripes you were born with, Bertie. And besides, do you know what you would be if you had more stripes? You would be a wasp!"

Bertie looked horrified. The last thing he wanted to be was a wasp. Wasps were always going around frightening and stinging everyone, and no-one liked them at all.

Bertie thought for a few moments and then said, "Perhaps having just a few stripes but being liked by others is better after all."

Bobby's Best Birthday Present

It was the morning of Bobby's birthday and he was very excited.
When he came down to breakfast, there on the table was a big
pile of presents. Bobby opened them one by one. There was a
beautiful book with pictures of wild animals, a toy racing car and
a baseball cap. Bobby was very pleased with his presents, but
where was the present from his parents? "Close your eyes and
hold out your hands!" said his mother. When he opened his eyes
there was a large rectangular parcel in his hands. Bobby tore off
the wrapping and inside was a box. And inside the box was a
wonderful, shiny, electric train set.

For a moment, Bobby looked at the train set lying in the box.
It was so lovely he could hardly bear to touch it. There was an
engine and six carriages all lying neatly on their sides. Bobby
carefully lifted the engine out of the box. Then he set up the
track and soon he had the train whizzing round his bedroom
floor. Freddie the cat came in and watched the train going
round. Round and round she watched it go, then one time when
the train came past her she swiped at it with her paw and
derailed it. The engine and the six carriages came tumbling off
the track and landed in a heap on the floor. "Look what you've
done!" wailed Bobby as he picked up the train and reassembled
it. The carriages were undamaged, but the engine had hit the
side of his bed and was badly dented.

Bobby was very upset. "My brand new train is ruined!" he cried.

"Don't worry, Bobby," said his mother, "we can't take it back to the store now, but we can take it to the toymender in the morning. I'm sure he'll make a good job of mending the engine and it'll look as good as new again." Bobby played with his racing car, he wore his new baseball cap and he read his new book, but really all he wanted to do was to play with his train set. He went to bed that night with the engine on the floor near his bed.

In the morning when Bobby woke up, the first thing he did was to look at the poor broken engine of his train set. He picked it up, expecting to see the buckled metal, but the engine was perfect. He couldn't believe his eyes! He ran to his parents. "Look, look!" he cried. They were as amazed as he was. The engine worked perfectly and Bobby played happily with his train set all day – but he made sure Freddie kept out of his room!

That night Bobby couldn't sleep. He lay in bed tossing and turning. Then he heard a noise. It was the sound of his train set rushing round the track. He peered into the darkness and yes, he could definitely make out the shape of the train as it sped by. How had the train started? It couldn't start all by itself! Had Freddie crept into his room and flicked the switch? As his eyes gradually became accustomed to the dark Bobby could make out several shapes in the carriages. Who were the mysterious passengers? He slid out of bed and on to the floor beside the train set. Now he could see that the passengers were little folk wearing strange pointed hats and leafy costumes. "Elves!" thought Bobby.

At that moment one of the elves spotted Bobby. "Hello there!" he called as the train rushed past again. "We saw that your train set was broken. We so much wanted a ride that we fixed it. I hope you don't mind!" Bobby was too astounded to say anything at all. "Come with us for a ride," called the elf as his carriage approached again.

As the train passed him the elf leaned out of the carriage and grabbed Bobby by the hand. Bobby felt himself shrinking as he flew through the air, and the next instant he was sitting beside the elf in the carriage of his very own train set! "Here we go – hold tight!" called the elf as the train left the track and went out through the window into the night sky.

"Now, where would you like to go? What would you like to see?" asked the elf.

"Toyland!" replied Bobby without hesitation. Sure enough, the train headed towards a track which curved up a mountain made of pink and white sugar. Beside the track were toys going about their daily business. Bobby saw a rag doll getting into a shiny tin car. Then a wooden sailor puppet wound up the car with a large key and off went the doll. He saw three teddy bears setting off for school with their satchels on their backs. Then he saw a brightly colored clown playing a drum.

The train stopped and Bobby and the elves got out. "Now for some fun!" said one of the elves. They had come to a halt by a toy fairground. Bobby found that this was like no other fairground he had ever been to before. For in Toyland, all the rides are real. The horses on the carousel were real horses. The dodgem cars were real cars. And when he got in the rocket for the rocket ride, it took him all the way to the moon and back!

"Time to go, Bobby," said one of the elves at last. "It'll be morning soon." Bobby climbed wearily back into the train and soon he was fast asleep. When he woke up it was morning, and he was back in his bed. The train set lay quite still on its tracks. But in one of the carriages was a scrap of paper and on the paper, in tiny spidery writing, were the words: *We hope you enjoyed your trip to Toyland – the elves.*

Little Red Riding Hood

There was once a little girl who was given a lovely, bright red cloak by her grandmother. The little girl loved this cloak very much. She loved it so much in fact that she never wanted to take it off, and was always wearing it. Because of this, she became known as Little Red Riding Hood.

One sunny morning, Little Red Riding Hood's mother asked her if she would take some cakes and apple juice to her grandmother, who was ill.

Little Red Riding Hood loved her grandmother very much, and was pleased to be going to visit her.

"But don't delay," said Little Red Riding Hood's
mother, "go straight to your grandmother's house
and don't play in the forest on the way."

Little Red Riding Hood promised to do as she
was told, and said goodbye to her mother and
set off.

On the way to her grandmother's house,
Little Red Riding Hood met a wolf walking
through the forest. Now Little Red Riding
Hood did not know that he was wicked, and
so she said, "Good morning, Mr Wolf."

"Well, good morning, Little Red Riding Hood,"
replied the wolf, "and where are you going?"

"I am going to visit my grandmother, who
is ill in bed," said Little Red Riding Hood.

"What have you got in your basket, Little Red Riding Hood?" asked the wolf.

"I've got some cakes and a jug of apple juice," said Little Red Riding Hood.

"And where does your grandmother live?" asked the wolf.

"She lives in the forest, not far from here," said Little Red Riding Hood. "Her house is easy to find. It's right next to the lake."

Now the reason that the wolf was asking all these questions was because he really wanted to gobble up Little Red Riding Hood and her grandmother. Suddenly he thought of a cunning plan. "Little Red Riding Hood," he said, "I have an idea! Why don't you pick some of those beautiful flowers which are growing in the forest and give them to your sick grandmother?"

"What a good idea," said Little Red Riding Hood. "My grandmother would be so pleased to have some of these pretty flowers. I'm sure they would make her feel better."

And with that, she set about picking a big bunch of the prettiest flowers she could find. In fact, she was so busy looking for flowers that she didn't see the crafty wolf skip away and make off towards her grandmother's house. The wolf soon came to the house, and knocked on the door.

"Who is it?" said Grandmother.

"It's me, Little Red Riding Hood," said the wolf. "I've brought you some cakes and a jug of apple juice."

"Come in, come in, my dear," said Grandmother, "the door isn't locked."

The wolf then went into the house, and as soon as he saw the old lady lying in bed, he ran straight over to her and gobbled her up. Next he put on her nightgown and her frilly night cap and jumped into her bed, pulling the comforter up to his chin.

In a little while, Little Red Riding Hood – who had by now picked a lovely bunch of flowers for her grandmother – came hurrying up the garden path. The door to her grandmother's house was still open and so she went inside and walked over to the bed. Little Red Riding Hood could only see a little bit of her face poking out from the comforter.

"My, Grandmother, what big ears you have," said Little Red Riding Hood.

24

"All the better to hear you with, my dear," said the wolf.

"My, Grandmother, what big eyes you have," said Little Red Riding Hood.

"All the better to see you with, my dear," said the wolf.

"My, Grandmother, what big hands you have," said Little Red Riding Hood.

"All the better to hold you tight with, my dear," said the wolf.

"My, Grandmother, what big teeth you have," said Little Red Riding Hood.

"All the better to eat you with, my dear," cried the wolf. And with that he jumped out of bed and gobbled her up.

The wolf felt very full and rather sleepy after he had eaten
Little Red Riding Hood. After all, he'd already
just eaten her grandmother, too. So he
went back to bed and fell
asleep, snoring loudly.

Just then, a hunter was passing the house and heard the
snoring. He looked through the window, and when he saw the
wolf lying in bed, he realized that the wolf must have eaten the
old lady. So, while the wolf was still sleeping, the hunter took his
knife and cut open the wolf's stomach. To the hunter's great
surprise, out popped Little Red Riding Hood and her
grandmother. Luckily, the hunter had arrived just in time and
both were still alive.

26

Little Red Riding Hood and her grandmother both thanked the hunter for saving them, and the hunter took the dead wolf's skin and went home.

Little Red Riding Hood's grandmother ate the cakes and drank the apple juice, and soon she was feeling much better. And Little Red Riding Hood? Well, she decided that she would never talk to a wolf again!

Mr Squirrel Won't Sleep

It was fall. The leaves were falling from the trees in the forest and there was a cold chill in the air. All the animals began to get ready for winter.

One night Mr Fox came back from hunting and said to his wife, "There's not much food about now it's getting colder. We'd better start storing what we can to help tide us over the winter."

"You're right, Mr Fox," replied his wife, as she gathered her cubs into their lair.

"I'd love to go fishing," said Mr Bear, "but I'll have to wait until spring now." He went into his den, shut the door tight and sealed it.

"Well, I'm off for a vacation in the sun," announced Mrs Cuckoo, preening her feathers. "See you all next year!" she called as she took to the wing and flew south.

Mrs Mouse ran by with a mouthful of straw. "Must dash," she squeaked, "or my winter bed will never be finished in time." But soon she, too, was curled up with her tail wrapped around her for warmth.

Now only Mr Squirrel wasn't ready for winter. He danced about in his tree, leaping from branch to branch and chasing his tail. "Ha, ha!" he boasted. "I don't have to get ready for winter. I have a fine store of nuts hidden away, a beautiful bushy tail to keep me warm and besides, I don't feel in the least bit sleepy." And he carried on playing in his tree.

"Are you still awake?" snapped Mr Fox.

"Go to sleep!" growled Mr Bear.

"Please be quiet," squeaked Mrs Mouse, drawing her tail more tightly about her ears.

But Mr Squirrel wouldn't go to sleep. Not a bit of it. He danced up and down all the more and shouted, "I'm having SUCH FUN!" at the top of his voice.

Winter came. The wind whistled in the trees' bare branches, the sky turned gray and it became bitterly cold. Then it started to snow. At first Mr Squirrel had a grand time making snowballs – but there was no-one around to throw them at and he began to feel rather lonely. Soon he felt cold and hungry, too.

"No problem!" he said to himself. "I'll have some nice nuts to eat. Now, where did I bury them?" He scampered down his tree to find that the ground was deep with snow. He ran this way and that trying to find his hiding places, but all the forest looked the same in the snow and soon he was hopelessly lost.

"Whatever shall I do?" he whimpered, for now he was shivering with cold and hunger and his beautiful, bushy tail was all wet and bedraggled.

All of a sudden he thought he heard a small voice. But where was it coming from? He looked all around but there was no sign of anyone. Then he realised that the voice was coming from under the snow. "Hurry up!" said the voice. "You can join me down here, but you'll have to dig a path to my door."

Mr Squirrel started digging frantically with his front paws and sure enough there was a path leading to a door under a tree stump. The door was slightly open – open enough for Mr Squirrel to squeeze his thin, tired body through.

Inside was a warm, cozy room with a roaring fire, and sitting by the fire was a tiny elf. "I heard you running around up there and thought you might be in need of a bit of shelter," said the elf. "Come and warm yourself by the fire." Mr Squirrel was only too pleased to accept and soon he was feeling warm and dry.

"This isn't my house, you know," said the elf. "I think it might be part of an old badgers' sett. I got lost in the forest and so when I found this place, I decided to stay here until spring. Though how I'll ever find my way home, I don't know." A fat tear rolled down the elf's cheek.

"I have been a very foolish squirrel," said Mr Squirrel. "If you hadn't taken me in I surely would have died. I am indebted to you and if you will let me stay here until spring, I will help you find your way home."

"Of course you can stay," replied the elf. "I'd be glad of the company." So Mr Squirrel settled down with his tail for a blanket and soon he was fast asleep.

Days and nights passed, until one day the elf popped his head out of the door and exclaimed, "The snow has melted, spring is coming. Wake up, Mr Squirrel." Mr Squirrel rubbed his eyes and looked out. It was true. There were patches of blue in the sky and he could hear a bird singing.

"Climb upon my back," Mr Squirrel said to the elf. "I'm going to show you the world." They set off through the forest until they came to the highest tree of all.

"Hold tight!" called Mr Squirrel as he climbed up through the branches until finally they reached the very top of the tree.

"You can look now," said Mr Squirrel, seeing that the elf had put his tiny hands over his eyes. The elf uncovered his eyes and stared and stared. He had never seen anything like it in his whole life. Stretching in all directions, as far as the eye could see, were mountains, lakes, rivers, forests and fields.

"What's that silvery-blue thing in the distance?" asked the elf.

"Why, that's the sea!" replied Mr Squirrel.

Suddenly the elf started to jump for joy.

"What is it?" said Mr Squirrel.

"I… I… can see my home," cried the elf, pointing down into the valley below the forest. "And there's my wife sitting in a chair in the sunshine. I must go home, Mr Squirrel. Thank you for showing me the world, for I should never have seen my home again without you." And with that he climbed down the tree and skipped all the way home.

Mr Squirrel made his way back to his own tree.

"Where have you been?" said Mr Fox.

"We've been looking for you," said Mr Bear.

"I'm glad you're home," said Mrs Mouse.

"So am I," said Mr Squirrel. "I've been very foolish, but I've learned my lesson. Now let's have a party – I've got rather a lot of nuts that need eating up!"

So the animals celebrated spring with a fine feast.

And Mr Squirrel vowed not to be silly again next winter.

The Bear and the Ice Kingdom

Once upon a time a king ruled a far-off land. It was a sunny, pleasant kingdom with lush forests, green meadows and sparkling rivers. The king of this land had a daughter he loved very much, and who one day would rule the kingdom.

Beyond the king's land was another kingdom, but this one was very different. It was an icy-cold place with wind-swept, snowy plains and cold, frozen seas. The sun never warmed this kingdom, and it was always winter. Anyone or anything venturing into the kingdom was immediately turned to ice by the cold. This kingdom was ruled by a wicked ogre, whose wish was to own the warm lands of his neighbor.

One day the wicked ogre thought of a cunning plan to capture the kingdom he desired. He decided he would kidnap the king's daughter. Once she had entered the wicked ogre's ice kingdom she, too, would be turned to ice. In time, the king would die and, as there would be no-one to inherit his kingdom, the wicked ogre could seize it.

So one day, the wicked ogre left his own cold kingdom and traveled to the other kingdom disguised as a merchant. He carried a big bag containing some samples of cloth and some jewelery. The wicked ogre came to the castle gates and asked if he might show the princess his wares. She agreed, and showed him to a room where he laid out the cloth and jewelery on a table. But as soon as she started to look at the wares, the wicked ogre bundled her up in the bag and carried her off.

As soon as the princess felt the cold chill of the wicked ogre's kingdom, she was immediately frozen to ice.

The wicked ogre thought that all he now had to do was wait for the king to die of old age or a broken heart, and the kingdom would be his. But despite the cunning of the wicked ogre, his evil deed had been spotted by one of the king's courtiers. The king immediately sent his troops to the ice kingdom to rescue his daughter. But as soon as they reached the kingdom they, too, were frozen to ice.

The king was in despair. There seemed to be no way to get his beloved daughter back. Then one day he thought of an idea. He sent out a royal proclamation to every part of his land. It said that anyone who could rescue his daughter would be granted any gift within the king's power to bestow.

Many adventurers tried to rescue the king's daughter, in the hope that they might win her hand in marriage, or be granted riches and lands as a reward. But each who ventured into the evil ogre's ice kingdom met the same fate. All were turned to ice.

Then one day, the king's dancing bear read the royal proclamation and asked to speak with the king. "Your majesty," said the dancing bear, "I have a plan to rescue your daughter, the princess."

"And what is your plan?" asked the king.

"My plan is a secret, your majesty," said the dancing bear. "But if you will trust me, I promise she will be brought safely home."

The king agreed to let the dancing bear try and rescue his daughter. After all, every other attempt had ended in failure so what did he have to lose? The dancing bear was released from his chain and went off immediately to begin his task. He traveled day and night until finally he reached his destination – a cold, snowy place where his cousin lived. His cousin was not like the dancing bear, however. The dancing bear was small and brown, but his cousin was big and white. This bear loved the cold and snow, for he had a thick fur coat. He was a polar bear.

The dancing bear told his cousin what had befallen the king's daughter. The polar bear agreed to rescue her. The dancing bear couldn't wait to get going, for his cousin's snowy home was much too cold for him. Eventually they arrived back in the king's land, and the polar bear set off alone to try and rescue the princess.

Soon he reached the wicked ogre's ice kingdom. A freezing, icy wind blew all around the polar bear, but his thick, warm fur coat kept out the cold. Then a huge snow storm came up, but the polar bear just shook his fur and all the snow fell from him. On went the polar bear until he reached the wicked ogre's castle.

The ogre never expected that anyone would be able to enter his cold kingdom without being turned to ice, so he never even locked his doors. While the ogre was snoring in his bedroom, the polar bear searched stealthily around the castle until he found the frozen princess. He gently gathered her up, and they were just about to make their escape when the ogre awoke.

As the wicked ogre tried to snatch the princess away from the polar bear, the polar bear dealt the wicked ogre a mighty blow with his paw. The wicked ogre fell down dead. The polar bear then carried the princess away from the icy kingdom. As soon as she entered her father's warm kingdom again, she returned to life.

There was much rejoicing at the return of the king's daughter, of course, and the first thing the king did was to summon the dancing bear to him.

"You have kept your promise," the king said, "and now I will keep mine. What is your wish?"

"All I ask, your majesty, is that I am freed to roam the forests of your kingdom."

The king immediately granted his wish. And as a reward to the polar bear, he was given the ice kingdom as his own domain which, being so cold, suited him just fine!

39

Jack and the Beanstalk

Once there was an old woman who lived with her only son Jack in a tumbledown cottage in a meadow by a pine forest. The old woman and her son were very poor, and they were getting poorer as each winter passed. After one particularly cruel and cold winter, when the ground had frozen like ice, the old woman turned to her son and said, "Jack, there is only one thing left to sell. You must take the old brown cow to market tomorrow and sell her for her meat – she is all that is left between us and starvation, so mind you get a good price!"

So the next morning Jack took the old brown cow and started the long journey into town.

Halfway through his journey, Jack stopped to eat his crust of bread. Just then a farmer passed by, and stopped to chat. After Jack told the farmer where he was heading and why, the farmer looked at the old cow and scratched his chin thoughtfully. He put his hand into his pocket and said to Jack, "I'll swap you these dried beans for your old brown cow."

Jack looked at the beans in the farmer's hand and shook his head. "I'm sorry," he said, "but I must take the old brown cow to sell at the market so that my mother and I can buy bread."

The farmer promised Jack that if he would swap the cow for the beans, Jack would make his fortune. Jack finally agreed, and went home with the beans in his pocket.

When he got home he told his mother about his adventure, but his mother cried when Jack told her the old brown cow was gone and all they had were dried beans. She snatched the beans from Jack's hand and threw them out of the window in anger.

41

Just as dawn was breaking, Jack woke up to discover a huge beanstalk had shot up during the night right outside his window. He ran downstairs and looked at the huge beanstalk – it was taller than even the tallest trees in the nearby pine forest, and disappeared into the clouds. Jack decided to climb the beanstalk.

Jack climbed and climbed. He climbed so high that when he looked down, the tumbledown cottage was a tiny speck far below. The top of the beanstalk was still out of sight so he climbed some more. Eventually, Jack climbed through the clouds and was amazed when he got to the top of the stalk to discover another land very different from the one he'd left below.

Everything was HUGE. The trees were enormous, the grass came up to Jack's shoulder, and in the distance was the largest castle he had ever seen. Just as Jack was starting out towards the castle, he heard a thunderous rustling in the grass behind him, and he looked round to see a huge giantess towering above him.

"Mmmmm – not much meat on those bones," she said, "so I won't bother to eat you. However, you might come in handy around the house to do all the boring old chores." And with that she picked Jack up and popped him into the pocket of her apron, and carried him into the castle. On the way, she warned Jack not to let her husband, the giant, see him. "The last house boy I had was made into jam, and he's looking for another to pound into bread," she said quite calmly.

Soon Jack felt the castle shudder at the approach of the giant, and he hid behind the coal scuttle. "Fee Fi Fo Fum," roared the giant. "I smell the blood of an Englishman. Be him live or be him dead, I'll break his bones to make my bread."

"Don't be silly," said the giantess, "you've never once changed your socks, and it's your feet you can smell."

Satisfied with this answer, the giant sat down and started to count his money. Jack sneaked a peek from his hiding place and saw a mountain of gold coins piled high on the table. Then the giant scooped it all back into a bag, put his feet on the table, and fell sound asleep.

43

When the thunderous snores convinced Jack that it was safe, he sneaked up on to the table. The bag was within reach, and Jack dragged it to the edge of the table where it fell with a tremendous KLUNK on to the floor. The giant slept on. Quickly Jack climbed down and dragged the bag to the castle door, and down to the meadow, and then down, down, down the beanstalk.

When Jack finally got back with his treasure he showed it to his mother who hugged him with joy, and warned him never to climb the beanstalk again.

But Jack decided that he would go back to the castle to find some more treasures, and when morning came again he got dressed and went down to the beanstalk to start the long climb all over again. Before he left the house, he tied a red scarf around his head, and painted freckles on his face, so that when he reached the top of the beanstalk and once again met the giantess, she would not recognize him.

44

Once again, she picked Jack up and popped him into her apron pocket, and warned him about the terrible giant. Once more, Jack hid as the castle trembled at the giant's approach.

"Fee Fi Fo Fum," roared the giant, "I smell the blood of an Englishman. Be him live or be him dead, I'll break his bones to make my bread."

"Tsk tsk," said the giantess, "the only thing you can smell is your armpits which have never been washed."

Satisfied with this answer, the giant sat down and called for his hen to be brought to him. Jack peeked around and saw to his amazement that the hen had laid a beautiful golden egg! Before long, the giant rested his head once more, then fell fast asleep.

When Jack heard the snoring, he sneaked up on to the table and gently took the hen, then quickly climbed down and carried it to the castle door, and down to the meadow and then down, down, down the beanstalk. When Jack returned once more with his treasure, his mother was waiting for him, and when Jack showed her the hen, she hugged him and begged him never to climb the beanstalk again.

But once again, Jack thought about the treasures in the castle, and the following morning he went down to the beanstalk to start the long climb all over again.

45

This time before he left the house, he tied a blue scarf around his head, and rubbed dirt into his face, and once again when he reached the top of the beanstalk and met the giantess, she did not recognize him. As before, she picked Jack up and popped him into her apron pocket, and warned him about the giant.

Again, the castle trembled at the approach of the giant. "Fee Fi Fo Fum. I smell the blood of an Englishman. Be him live or be him dead, I'll break his bones to make my bread," said the giant once again.

"What rot!" said the giantess. "That'll be all those bugs in your hair that's never been combed!"

Once more satisfied, the giant sat down and called for his harp to be brought to him. When the giant plucked at the strings of the harp, it magically started to sing in a clear soprano voice! The giant was soon lulled into a deep slumber across the table, and Jack wanted the beautiful harp so much that he didn't even wait for the snores! Jack climbed up to the table and put his hands on the harp to sneak it from under the nose of the sleeping giant, but to his horror, the harp started to shriek, "Help! Help! I'm being stolen."

The giant woke up. With a mighty roar he shouted, "Fee Fi Fo Fum, I smell the blood of an Englishman. Be him live or be him dead, I'll break his bones to make my bread." And with that he raced after Jack. But the giant wasn't as nimble as Jack, and Jack was able to rush out of the castle, down to the meadow and reach the top of the beanstalk with the giant in pursuit. Jack climbed down as quickly as possible, but the giant was not far behind him. The further down Jack climbed, the closer the giant got to him. When Jack was nearly at the bottom, he called to his mother to fetch the wood axe, and then Jack jumped the rest of the way to the ground. He grabbed at the axe and started to chop furiously at the stalk. The giant was almost down when the beanstalk crashed to the ground – right on top of him! The giant was squashed to nothing.

Now, with all the gold they had, Jack and his mother never needed to worry about money again.

This is a Dempsey Parr Book
Dempsey Parr is an imprint of Parragon

Parragon
Queen Street House
4 Queen Street
Bath BA1 1HE

Written by Derek Hall, Alison Morris and
Louisa Somerville
Illustrated by Lynn Breeze, Anna Cattermole,
Maureen Galvani, Mary Hall, Paula Martyr,
Martin Orme and Jenny Williams

Printed and bound in Spain
ISBN 1-84084429-9